W9-AAJ-339

The Sneaky Snow Fox

Patricia Reilly Giff

ILLUSTRATED BY **Diane Palmisciano**

ORCHARD BOOKS • NEW YORK

AN IMPRINT OF SCHOLASTIC INC.

For Arlene Weber Callahan, with love—P.R.G.

In memory of M.P. and G.B.—D.V.P.

Text copyright © 2012 by Patricia Reilly Giff
Illustrations copyright © 2012 by Diane Palmisciano

All rights reserved. Published by Orchard Books, an imprint of Scholastic Inc., *Publishers since 1920.*
ORCHARD BOOKS and design are registered trademarks of Watts Publishing Group, Ltd., used under license.
SCHOLASTIC and associated logos are trademarks and/or registered trademarks of Scholastic Inc.

No part of this publication may be reproduced, stored in a retrieval system, or transmitted in any form or by any means, electronic, mechanical, photocopying, recording, or otherwise, without written permission of the publisher. For information regarding permission, write to Orchard Books, Scholastic Inc., Permissions Department, 557 Broadway, New York, NY 10012.

Library of Congress Cataloging-in-Publication Data
Giff, Patricia Reilly.
The sneaky snow fox / by Patricia Reilly Giff ; illustrated by Diane Palmisciano. — 1st ed. p. cm. — (Fiercely and friends)
Summary: When her pet dog goes outside during a snow storm, an imaginative young girl tries to save him from the sneaky snow fox.
ISBN 978-0-545-24458-9 (hardcover : alk. paper)—ISBN 978-0-545-43378-5 (lib. bdg. : alk. paper) [1. Imagination—Fiction. 2. Snow—Fiction. 3. Dogs—Fiction.] I. Palmisciano, Diane, ill. II. Title. III. Series.
PZ7.G3626Snj 2012 [E]—dc23 2011025324

10 9 8 7 6 5 4 3 2 1 12 13 14 15 16

Printed in Malaysia 108
Reinforced Binding for Library Use
First edition, November 2012

The display type was set in P22Parrish Roman. The text was set in Garamond Premier Pro.
The art was created using oil pastels.
Book design by Chelsea C. Donaldson

CONTENTS

A Scary Story

"Watch out! Here comes the fox!"
I was reading to Fiercely
from my new book.
My voice was shivery.
Fiercely was afraid.

He chewed the corner of the couch.

No wonder.

It was a scary story about a sly, sneaky fox.

The fox sneaked through the snow.

He snipped and snapped his teeth.

I put the book down.

I was afraid to keep reading.

Outside, wind *whooshed*
across the yard.
The house shook.
So did I.
Suppose a fox was out there
in the snow?

Fiercely licked ice away from the window.
We had to see.
Next door, the Big Red Schoolhouse
was a Big White Schoolhouse.

Burt's Bookstore
was just around the block.
Was it buried in the snow, too?
Poor Burt and Mimi, his cat,
and all those books I wanted to read.

“It’s a blizzard,” I told Fiercely.
“We’ll ski down the street
and shovel Burt out.”
Too bad. I had no skis.
I had no shovel, either.

Wait.

What was moving through

all that white?

I tried to see.

It had pointy ears.

It had a fat tail, too.

It looked *DANGEROUS* to me.

Fiercely agreed. He jumped into my arms.

"It's a snow fox!" I told Fiercely.

"Sneaky, with terrible teeth.

Maybe he ate dogs for supper.

Maybe he ate kids, too!"

I pulled down the shade.
The snow fox couldn't see in.
But Fiercely chewed a hole
in the edge.
Now he could see out.

Downstairs, something banged
on the door.
It banged hard.
Fiercely barked louder
than the banging door!
I covered my ears.

“Don’t open it,” I told Nana.
But Nana was dusting
the cobwebs on the stairs.
“See who it is, Jilli,” she said.

I went downstairs.

I closed one eye.

Then I opened the front door two inches.

I took a small peek.

Something was covered in snow.

Was it the snow fox

snipping and snapping . . . *at me*?

Not the Fox!

It was my friend Jim.

He was covered with snow.

“I have two skis,” he said.

“There’s one ski for you,

and one ski for me.”

“Have you seen a snow fox?” I asked.
Jim looked worried.
“Does it have pointy ears
and a fat tail?”
“Yes.” I held my breath.
“Not today,” he said.

Fiercely was still barking
ENORMOUSLY.
Jim gave him a dog biscuit
covered with snow.
Fiercely loved to eat dog biscuits.
He loved to eat snow, too.

Jim came in.

So did a *whoosh* of snow!

Fiercely raced out with his biscuit.

"Fiercely, please come back,"
I called.
But Fiercely never listened!
Now he was lost in the snow.
Just like Burt's Bookstore.

Jim took off his snowy things.

We raced upstairs to the window.

We peeked out the Fiercely hole.

A million snowflakes
were coming down.
I could just see
Fiercely's back paws.
Ahead of him, I saw a fat tail.
It must be that sneaky fox!
And what was Fiercely doing?

"He's digging a snow tunnel,"
Jim said.
I nodded. "Yes, he's going
straight for the fox."
"That dog is brave," Jim said.

But Fiercely wasn't brave at all!
He hid in the tub
when the mailman came.
He slid under the bed
when he heard thunder!

And suppose the sneaky fox
turned and saw Fiercely!
He might eat him
from his head to his skinny tail.
"We have to save Fiercely," I said.

To the Rescue

I led Jim up to the closet.
I found my tiger outfit.
Jim put on the tiger hat.
I put on the boots
with the tiger feet.

We put on our jackets and raced outside.
"Look out, snow fox!" I said.
"Here come the tigers!"
And Jim said, "Wait till he sees us
on these skis!"
Jim put on one ski.
I put on the other.

"Tell Burt I said hello," Nana called.

We waved to Nana.

We skied down the street.

Swish. Clump. Swish. Clump.

"There goes the snow fox!" Jim yelled.

"And Fiercely is right behind him."

"Come back, Fiercely!" I called.

"Please don't let the snow fox eat you!"

The snow stopped.
The Big Red Schoolhouse
looked red again.

We skied past the school.
We skied past Sarah's Seed Shop.
We skied past Ralph's This and That.

We skied past Burt's Bookstore.
Burt opened the door
and waved to us.
But where was the sneaky snow fox?
Where was Fiercely?

Burt's Bookstore

Suddenly, we stopped!

We saw a skinny tail.

We saw a fat tail, too.

"Fiercely!" I cried.

"Sneaky Snow Fox!" cried Jim.

"*RUFF!*" cried Fiercely.

"*MEOW!*" said the sneaky snow fox.

It wasn't a snow fox.

It wasn't even a fox.

It was Mimi, the bookstore cat.

"What's all that ruckus?" Burt asked.
"It's just Fiercely and Mimi," I said.
"It's not a snow fox at all."

"Come on in, tigers," Burt said.
"Leave your skis outside."
We followed Burt into his shop.
"I have the perfect book for you,"
he said. "I baked cookies, too!"

“Take off your snowy things,” Burt said.
“Don’t worry about puddles.”

We sat on the bookstore stools.

Fiercely and Mimi lay down on the floor.

Burt opened up a book.

“Hey,” I said. “I know that book!

But I was afraid to finish it.”

Burt began to read.
"Once there was a sneaky snow fox
who snipped and snapped his teeth."
In the end, he sneaked home to his mother.
She read him a scary story about
a girl and a boy and a dog.
"Just like us," I told Jim.
"*Woof!*" Fiercely agreed.